THE *DIARY OF A WIMPY KID* SERIES

MORE FROM THE *WIMPY* WORLD

DIARY
of a
Wimpy Kid

NO BRAINER

by Jeff Kinney

AMULET BOOKS

New York

Cataloging-in-Publication Data has been applied for and may be obtained from the Library of Congress.

ISBN 978-1-4197-6694-7

Book design by Jeff Kinney
Cover design by Jeff Kinney with Pamela Notarantonio and Lora Grisafi

Printed and bound in U.S.A.
10 9 8 7 6 5 4 3 2 1

Amulet Books are available at special discounts when purchased in quantity for premiums and promotions as well as fundraising or educational use. Special editions can also be created to specification. For details, contact specialsales@abramsbooks.com or the address below.

ABRAMS The Art of Books
195 Broadway, New York, NY 10007
abramsbooks.com

TO MATT

Monday

The human brain is supposed to be this amazing supercomputer that's capable of all sorts of incredible stuff. But if that's true, then I don't know why my brain is always making me do stupid things.

It's actually a little annoying, because if you think about it, your brain's one job is to be smart.

I guess it's my own fault for filling my brain with things that aren't important, like video game cheat codes and theme songs to old TV shows. Because now there's no room left for stuff that actually matters.

The problem with a brain is that there's only a limited amount of room in there, so eventually you run out of storage. And the reason it's hard for old people to learn new things is because their brains are just full.

One of these days they're gonna figure out a way to add more memory. And when they do, I'm gonna buy myself the biggest booster pack I can afford.

In the meantime, I'm trying to be real choosy about what I put in my brain. So when someone's telling me something I don't need to know, I just try and block it out.

When you're a kid, the thing that you use your brain for the most is school. And a lot of your brain power goes to memorizing useless stuff, like the names of vice presidents and the words to preschool songs.

One thing that's really inconvenient is that your brain is inside your head, so you have to take it everywhere you go. But if they ever figure out a way to deal with that issue, then school is gonna be a whole different thing.

I think it would be great if your brain could be at school learning while you're off doing things you actually enjoy, like playing laser tag with your friends or hanging out at the arcade. Then you could pick up your brain at the end of the day and get all caught up.

For now I guess we're stuck with the current situation where your body and your brain need to be in the same place. And if you're a kid, that means you've gotta spend a big chunk of your time at school.

My problem with that is how long the school day is.

You're there for seven hours, but you probably only spend twenty minutes a day on actual learning. And that's because most of your time is spent on stuff that doesn't have anything to do with education.

Today in fifth period we spent zero time learning about History because a bee got loose in the classroom. And that pretty much killed the chance of anything productive happening.

I wish everyone would stop fooling around and just get down to business once school starts.

Because that way we could get the learning part over with and be out of there before lunchtime. But I think they like to stretch things out and keep you there for as long as possible.

The whole reason school was invented in the first place is because back in olden times, kids were causing too many problems at home while their parents were at work.

TWANG

THWOCK

So they created this whole system with textbooks and lockers and Algebra and Phys Ed just to keep kids out of trouble for a few hours every day.

You're in school from the time you're four until you're at least eighteen. And after you're done with your education, you have to get a job and work until you reach old age. So by the time you're through with all that, you're too tired to do anything fun.

If they really wanted to, they could probably teach you everything you actually need to know by the time you're five or six. But I guess parents don't want to have to compete with their kids for good-paying jobs.

So they teach you a little bit at a time so you don't get too smart too quick. And sometimes they teach you stuff you can't even USE.

That's what's been happening at my school lately. I just took three months of Latin with a teacher named Mr. Leyton, and it was my favorite class. But it turns out he didn't know Latin at all, and was teaching us nonsense the whole time.

When the school found out Mr. Leyton was a fraud, they fired him. So now all I've got to show for the last three months of my life is knowing how to order a hamburger in a language that doesn't even exist.

Mr. Leyton isn't the only one teaching us stuff we can't really use. My Social Studies teacher is Mrs. Lackey, and this is her last year. So the only countries she teaches us about are the ones she's planning on visiting with her husband after she retires.

And for our last homework assignment, she had us research which cruise ships have the best meal plans.

	FREE DRINKS	GLUTEN-FREE MENU	DESSERT BAR	SALAD BAR
PREMIERE CRUISE LINE	X	X	X	X
QUEEN CRUISES		X		
ISLAND HOPPER		X		X

Some of our teachers don't even bother trying to teach us anything at all. Ms. Pritchard is supposed to be teaching us Geometry, but she uses her new smart board for stuff like helping her pick out which breed of puppy to get.

A few of the teachers are doing their best, but us kids don't always make it easy for them. Mr. Rask tried teaching Science the regular way for half the year, but nobody seemed interested.

So he switched to teaching about gross stuff.
And even though it makes Science a lot more
interesting, I don't think any of the information
we're learning right now is gonna help us get into
a good college later on.

I wish I didn't know half the stuff I've learned
in Mr. Rask's class. Because ever since we watched
a video about the microscopic parasites living on our
skin, I can't stop itching.

We don't even have an Algebra teacher anymore. Mrs. Kwan went on maternity leave back in October, and they never found a long-term sub to fill in for her.

So during fourth period they just stick us in a computer lab and have us go on this math-game website, which is sponsored by a candy company.

Now everyone in my grade needs candy to do math, and when we took a standardized test last month, a bunch of kids brought packs of jelly beans and bubble gum to help them count.

I probably would've done a lot better on the test if I wasn't sitting behind a kid who went through an entire jar of Gobsmashers.

It wasn't just the math section that was hard, though.

14

The reading section had a bunch of essays, and the science section had questions about stuff we never covered in class. And there wasn't a single question about farts or burps.

So when our school's test results came back, it wasn't a surprise that our scores were the lowest in the state. In fact, our scores were so bad we made the news.

TEST SCORES PLUMMET

MIDDLE SCHOOL'S PERFORMANCE NOSE-DIVES

A lot of parents were pretty upset, including mine. And I guess the superintendent was under pressure to make big changes, because he fired our principal, Mrs. Mancy, and asked the old principal, Mr. Bottoms, to come out of retirement.

I'm actually surprised Mr. Bottoms agreed to come back, because the way my older brother Rodrick described it, when Mr. Bottoms retired a few years ago, he went out with a bang.

But I'm rooting for him to turn things around. Because based on my education so far, the only job I'm gonna be qualified for is a cruddy middle-school Latin teacher.

<u>Friday</u>
Principal Bottoms has only been in charge for a few days, but he's already made some big changes. And any class that doesn't teach stuff that's on the standardized test has been cut.

Which kind of stinks, because we had just started the Brownie Baking unit in our Home Ec class.

Things have gotten a lot more serious in the classes that weren't cut, like Science. Mr. Rask isn't teaching about body smells and things like that anymore, but that doesn't mean the stuff we're learning isn't gross. Because this week he announced we were starting a Dissection unit on tapeworms.

17

Luckily, there weren't enough tapeworms to go around, so me and my partner, Tyler Geary, had to work with some noodles from the cafeteria instead. Tyler takes this science stuff pretty seriously, though, and you'd never think he was operating on leftover pasta.

I guess maybe Tyler will grow up to be a surgeon one day. But I hope I don't end up on his operating table, because I'll know exactly where he got his education.

Everybody thinks learning science is great, but they never talk about the flip side of things. I've seen a bunch of movies where a scientist loses their mind and tries to take over the world. But you never see any movies where the villain is a mad zookeeper or a mad gardener.

So when it comes to science, I think the less you know, the better. Because I don't need to be the guy who messes around and accidentally opens up a portal to the demon realm.

SCREAMMM!

Tyler Geary says that if we ever get to operate on real tapeworms, he's gonna try to bring one back to life by hooking it up to electrodes. And this is exactly the type of thing I'm worried about.

If you ask me, you shouldn't go screwing around trying to bring the dead back to life. On top of it just being wrong, it could also be pretty awkward.

I feel bad I never sent my Great Aunt Reba a thank-you card for the birthday money she gave me a few years ago. So I don't know what I'd say to her if she was back in the picture all of a sudden.

SORRY, I COULDN'T FIND STAMPS!

HISSSS!

When I'm gone, I hope my family doesn't try and bring ME back to life. Because if coming back means having to babysit my great-great-great grandkids, I'd rather everyone just let me rest in peace.

But I probably shouldn't worry about someone in my class making a big scientific breakthrough, because you need the proper equipment for that sort of thing. And my school can't even afford to give everyone the right kind of protective eyewear, so people have been bringing their own gear from home.

The science lab isn't the only place in our school that doesn't have the proper equipment, though.

Half the laptops in the computer center have missing letters on their keyboards. And last week I got a bad grade on a History paper when I had to use a computer that was missing all the vowels.

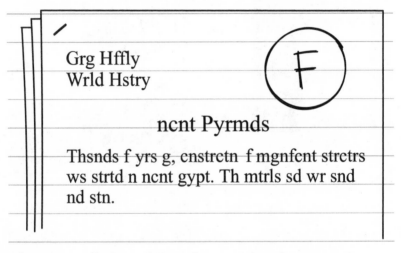

Grg Hffly
Wrld Hstry

F

ncnt Pyrmds

Thsnds f yrs g, cnstrctn f mgnfcnt strctrs ws strtd n ncnt gypt. Th mtrls sd wr snd nd stn.

The area of the school where we're shortest on materials is the library, because a lot of the shelves are empty. But it wasn't always like that.

Back in September we got a new librarian named Ms. Masie, who created a graphic novel section and filled it with books she paid for with her own money.

The most popular books were from this series called Commando Crocodile, and no matter how many copies she bought, Ms. Masie couldn't keep them on the shelves. If you wanted to check out a copy, you had to put your name on a list that was a mile long.

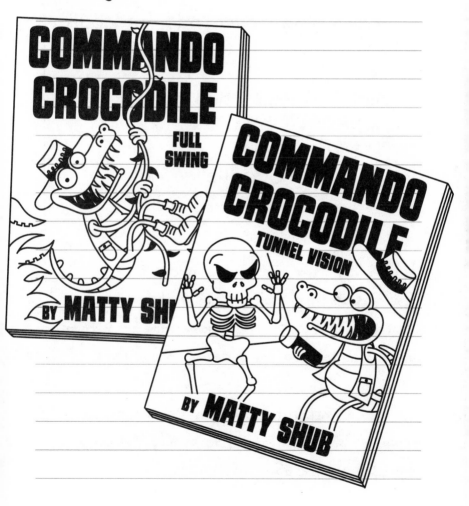

But I guess some parent had a problem with the way Commando Crocodile was drawn, so they filled out a complaint form.

Library Book Challenge Form

Name of Book: Commando Crocodile: Tunnel Vision

Author: Matty Shub

Reason for challenge:
crocodile is not wearing pants

Apparently, the rule is that if one parent complains about a book, it has to be removed from the library. But Ms. Masie came up with a compromise to keep the series on the shelves.

She used a marker to draw pants on Commando Crocodile, and that seemed to satisfy the parent who made a stink about it.

But then a new problem cropped up. Some kids had their own uncensored copies of Commando Crocodile at home, and they brought them to school. And when Principal Bottoms found out about it, he confiscated their copies.

25

So then the school started checking our bags for Commando Crocodile books at the beginning of the day, which added fifteen minutes to get through the doors.

But kids are smart, and some of them figured out ways to sneak the books into school anyway.

It turns out that complaints are contagious, because some parents suddenly noticed that there were a bunch of books in the library that had animals without ANY clothes, so then Ms. Masie had to spend her time dealing with THAT issue.

Eventually, Ms. Masie gave up and put all the books that were challenged in a back room. And if you wanted to read them you had to get a permission slip from a parent.

After a while, there were more books in the banned section than the main library, so the school had to write to all the parents and ask them to donate books from home.

But that just gave everyone an excuse to unload all the books they didn't want.

If you ask me, I think the whole book-banning thing backfired. A lot of people donated romance novels, and the stuff in them is a lot more inappropriate than anything in Commando Crocodile.

My mom says those types of books aren't real literature, but I figure as long as a person is reading, it's a good thing.

<u>Wednesday</u>

Principal Bottoms is trying to encourage kids to get better grades, so last week he created this new program called the High Flyers Club, which is kind of like one of those airline rewards programs. The basic idea is that the better you do in school, the more rewards you earn.

The kids in the High Flyers Club get all sorts of perks, like preferred seating in the classrooms with extra legroom.

WRIGGLE
WRIGGLE

But that kind of stinks for the rest of us,
because now there's less space for everyone else.

In Geometry, there wasn't a lot of room to begin
with, so to make extra space for the High Flyers,
they had to take out a whole row of seats.

That means kids like me who used to sit in the back
row have to sit on the heater. And that thing is
so hot that if you stay still too long, your butt
could burst into flames. So I have to shift from
one cheek to the other to give each a break.

HOT HOT
HOT!

But extra legroom isn't the only thing we're jealous about. The High Flyers get snacks and drinks during class, which they're not allowed to share with the rest of us.

When they're not in class, the High Flyers get to use the teachers' lounge. And I've heard the teachers aren't too thrilled with that part of the deal.

I'm not too bothered that those kids can use the teachers' lounge, but I am jealous they get to use the bathroom in there. I've heard it's a one-seater, and I really need my privacy when I go.

The High Flyers even have their own separate entrance when they get to school, so they breeze through security in the morning.

On top of that, the High Flyers get let out of school before everyone else. And even though it's only five minutes early, that's still plenty of time to get a head start on the bullies.

Everyone wants to be a part of the High Flyers Club, but it's not easy to get in. You need to have straight A's in all your classes, and there are only a handful of kids smart enough to actually pull that off.

So some kids have been cheating to try and get better grades. And they've been coming up with some pretty ingenious ways to do it, too.

In Geometry, Adam Katz wrote a bunch of equations on the back of the sticker on his water bottle so he could look at them during a test. And he might've gotten away with it if he wasn't so obvious about what he was doing.

In Science, a kid named Damon Fell actually made a fake arm, which he put on top of his desk during the test. Then he looked up answers on the phone he was holding UNDERNEATH the desk. The only reason he got busted was because he got a notification in the middle of the test.

DING!

Some kids have been teaming up to cheat. A few girls in my History class wrote the names of the most important battles of the Civil War on the backs of their necks, then moved their hair out of the way once the test started.

And in English, a bunch of kids created this crazy system of communicating answers to each other by using Morse code with their pens, but nobody let me in on what they were up to.

The cheating's become such a big problem that today the school had an assembly to deal with it.

They brought in this guy named Clarence Cluster, who said he started cheating when he was in middle school, which ruined his whole life. And I think his story actually shook a few kids up.

But I'm 90% sure that this guy's name wasn't even Clarence Cluster, and he was just an actor the school brought in to scare us.

That's because he looked exactly like one of the characters in a dinner theater show my family went to over the summer.

If the school really wanted to get through to us about how dishonesty can ruin your life, they should've brought in the school's very first principal, Larry Mack. But I guess they couldn't do that, since he's still in prison.

If the name Larry Mack sounds familiar, it's because his family owns a giant chain of car dealerships out on Route One.

And he's still on a bunch of old billboards nobody ever bothered to take down.

But Larry Mack didn't start off in the car business. He was the principal of the middle school for ten years, and after he got famous for his car dealerships they named the school after him.

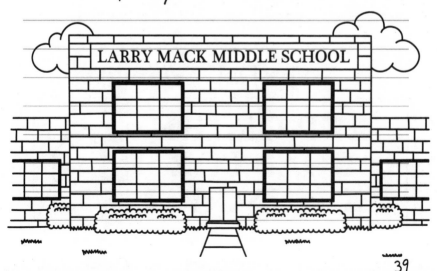

He was so popular that they even made a statue of him, which they put in the front courtyard.

But after Larry Mack opened his fifth car dealership, some reporters started poking around, trying to learn how he got the money to start his business. With a little detective work, they figured out he'd been stealing from the middle school for years. And it was a huge scandal at the time.

The Daily Herald

END OF THE ROAD FOR EX-PRINCIPAL

LARRY MACK

From what I heard, the police arrested him at his dealership, right in the middle of a sale.

After that, the school took down the statue, or at least the Larry Mack part of it. The only evidence that he was ever there is his shoes, which they couldn't get off the pedestal.

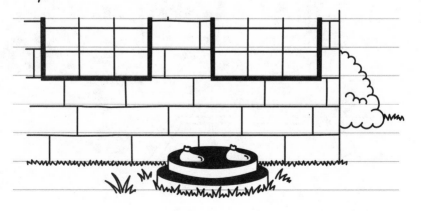

They never did change the name of the school, though. And I think that's because some people like being linked to someone famous, even if that person's famous for doing a terrible thing.

You'd think people in my town would be embarrassed to have their middle school named after a crook, but nobody around here seems too bothered by it. Even the school mascot, the Looter, was inspired by Larry Mack.

The fact that Larry Mack landed in prison didn't stop him from making money, though.

He wrote an autobiography, which apparently sold a ton of copies. I know my school bought at least fifty of them, because they take up two whole shelves in the Larry Mack section of the library.

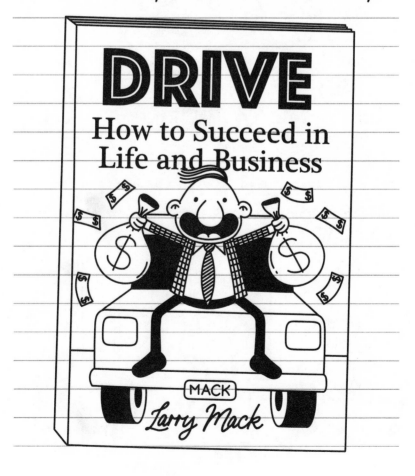

A kid named Albert Sandy who sits at my lunch table said that Larry Mack only used HALF the money he stole to start his car dealership, and he buried the other half under the school.

That got everyone all stirred up, and people started bringing in tools from home to try and find Larry Mack's secret treasure.

DINK DINK

CLONK

CLINK CLINK

Last week, this kid named Danny Tang got the idea that the money could be hidden in the WALLS. So he broke a hole through the back of his locker to see if he could find anything.

Unfortunately for me, Danny's locker is on the other side of MINE, and now there's nothing between them.

To make things worse, kids figured out that the hole between our lockers was a shortcut from the A wing to the B wing of the school. So now whenever I open my locker between classes, there's always a line of kids waiting to get through.

Danny decided to try and make a little money off the situation, and he started charging people to take the shortcut through his locker. So that gave some other kids the idea to create shortcuts of their OWN.

But not every locker connects to one on the other side. And Christian McKay found out the hard way that his locker shares a wall with the principal's private bathroom.

After that, Principal Bottoms put his foot down, so now we're not allowed to bring any kind of digging tools to school, which means it takes TWICE as long to get through security in the morning.

SHAKE
SHAKE

CLANK

<u>Friday</u>

It turns out Principal Bottoms was only getting started with the new rules, because now there are a BUNCH of them.

The latest rule is that if you're in the hallway while class is in session, you need to have a hall pass. And I can kind of see why Principal Bottoms made that change, because sometimes it seems like there are more kids in the hallways than there are in the classrooms.

But as soon as Principal Bottoms came up with that rule, kids just started making their OWN hall passes, and the hall monitors couldn't tell which ones were fake and which were real.

So Principal Bottoms made a new rule that every teacher had to have their own unique hall pass that wouldn't be easy for us kids to fake. Now Madame Lefrere's hall pass is a big French-English dictionary, and Mr. Ball's hall pass is his used size-fourteen basketball shoe.

Mr. Rask's hall pass is a human skeleton, which you attach to your wrist with rubber bands.

I've decided it's not even worth asking Mr. Rask if you can use the bathroom during his class, because the whole experience is just way too embarrassing.

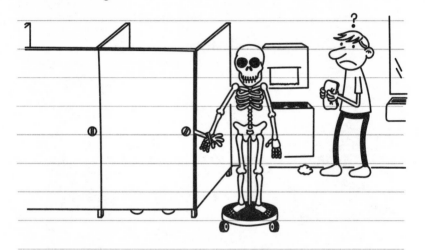

Speaking of the bathroom, there's a new rule about how long you're allowed to actually be in there.

Apparently, teachers were complaining that kids were hanging out in the bathrooms too long, so the new deal is that you're supposed to be in and out of there within a minute. They even had a whole assembly on how to get everything done in sixty seconds.

It's one thing to make a rule, but it's another thing to enforce it. The school appointed a handful of kids to be bathroom monitors, and gave them whistles and stopwatches and everything.

But all the bathroom monitors ended up quitting, because it turns out people don't like being rushed when they're trying to use the facilities.

Once the monitors were gone, kids hung out in the bathrooms longer than ever. Chris Kodiak, whose dad is a barber, even started up his own little business in the A-wing boys' room.

The school ended up removing the mirrors from ALL the bathrooms to get us to hurry things along. And now I have to rely on my best friend Rowley to tell me if I've got something in my nose.

BOOGER CHECK!

I don't know what it's like in the girls' bathroom, but in the guys' bathroom it's just a total zoo. And I guess the reason is because it's the only place in the school that's unsupervised by adults.

Every once in a while, though, one of the male teachers will pop their head in and tell everyone to quit horsing around.

But in the B wing, all the teachers are women, so the boys know they can totally go nuts in the bathroom without anybody coming in to tell them to cut it out. And it gets so crazy that I won't even go in there unless it's urgent.

I heard that recently things got so out of hand in the B-wing bathroom that Mrs. Lackey had to go inside to put a stop to it. But she had to wear a blindfold so she didn't violate anyone's privacy, which meant nobody actually got in any trouble.

After that, things were worse than ever.

On Wednesday, Justin Murdock got called down to the principal's office for writing on the bathroom wall with a marker. And on Thursday, Jorge Cantos got in trouble for hanging from one of the stalls and bending the frame.

Justin and Jorge both got detention, and all the guys became paranoid because they thought someone had to be a snitch.

But eventually they figured out how they were getting busted.

There's a metal paper towel dispenser in the B-wing bathroom, and if you're in the hallway you can see what's going on by looking at the reflection. So that's how the teachers busted Justin and Jorge for doing what they did.

The thing is, the reflection is blurry, so even though the teachers can KIND of see what's going on in the bathroom, it's not perfect. And that's how I got sent to the principal's office for something I didn't even do.

Principal Bottoms said a teacher reported me for breaking the handle off a urinal. And I know for a fact that the kid who actually did that was Marty Vinson, because I overheard him bragging about it in the cafeteria.

But I wasn't gonna snitch on Marty Vinson, since he's the kind of kid who can make your life miserable. So I just sat there and took it while Principal Bottoms chewed me out for being a vandal.

Principal Bottoms made me fill out a self-evaluation form, which is another one of his new policies.

All I can say is, I hope this doesn't end up on my permanent record, because I've already got enough bad stuff on there as it is.

LARRY MACK MIDDLE SCHOOL

Self-Evaluation Form

Nature of infraction:

broken urinal handle

How did this happen?

no clue

How did this make your classmates feel?

They thought it was pretty hilarious

How can you avoid this kind of behavior in the future?

be more gentle when flushing

<u>Thursday</u>

I guess Principal Bottoms finally went a little too
far with the new rules, because kids are starting
to push back. But this isn't about hall passes or
bathroom rules. This is about fudgedogs.

If you've never heard of fudgedogs before, it's
because my school is the only place you can get
them. And that's because they were invented here.

It actually happened by accident. Last year, the
school tried introducing some healthier options at
lunch, and they replaced beef hot dogs with tofu
ones. And let's just say they weren't a big hit
with the students.

The school had hundreds of uneaten tofu dogs, and they were planning on just throwing them all away.

But when a cafeteria lady named Mrs. Podsner dumped the tofu dogs in the trash, one of them fell into a vat of hot fudge that was being mixed for that day's ice cream sundae bar.

I guess she got curious, so Mrs. Podsner took a bite of the fudge-covered tofu dog. And when she did she knew she had just invented a whole new food type.

A few days later, fudgedogs were officially on the menu. And from the moment they went on sale in the cafeteria, they were a smash hit.

In fact, they were so popular that kids in the first two lunch periods were buying up all the fudgedogs and reselling them at a higher price to the kids who had lunch later on. And Ricky Fisher made a killing doing that.

Cafeteria sales went up 60%, and the school even held an assembly where Mrs. Podsner got the recognition she deserved.

Now there are Fudgedog Fridays, where it's buy two and get one free. And you can get all sorts of toppings at the fudgedog station, like rainbow sprinkles and miniature marshmallows.

The school even held a Fall Fudgedog Festival where there were all sorts of fudgedog-themed activities for the whole family.

Me and Rowley entered the fudgedog tower competition, but once we got ours four feet high, the whole thing collapsed.

63

Other schools in the area heard about our fudgedogs and tried to create their own. But apparently they used beef hot dogs, and it wasn't the same.

Some kids from Slacksville actually broke into our school on a Sunday night to try and steal our secret recipe. But luckily Mrs. Podsner was working late making that week's batch of fudgedogs, and she caught them in the act.

Fudgedogs have become such a big deal at our school that we recently replaced our old mascot with one named Fudgy. And now other schools hate coming to our gym to play us in basketball.

SQUIRT

People around here just love their fudgedogs. So you can probably imagine how shocked everyone was to come to school and find out fudgedogs had been canceled.

SORRY, KIDS, NO FUDGE-DOGS

Principal Bottoms was the person who made the decision. The school hired some company to help figure out why test scores had fallen so sharply, and their answer was that fudgedogs were at the root of it.

Apparently, visits to the nurse's office have skyrocketed ever since fudgedogs were introduced, and kids have been missing a ton of class time.

I've never personally gotten sick from eating a fudgedog, but I'll admit that whenever I have more than one, I don't feel like I'm at my best. And a lot of kids have gotten into the habit of taking a nap right after lunch, especially on Fudgedog Fridays.

Even though everyone knows fudgedogs probably aren't good for you, it was still a shock when they got discontinued. And on Monday, students staged a walkout to protest the decision.

Principal Bottoms tried to calm things down by introducing a new "fun food" to the menu, and Fudgedog Fridays got replaced with Macaroni Mondays.

The school even put posters up in the hallways to try and get kids excited.

But serving a bunch of angry middle schoolers macaroni was just asking for trouble.

Things got so out of control that Principal Bottoms had to meet with the student council to see if they could come up with a solution together.

Principal Bottoms said he'd allow fudgedogs back on the menu as long as kids only had one apiece. But the student council said that was too harsh, and the limit should be two per person.

So they split the difference and landed on one and a half fudgedogs per student per day. And even though nobody was completely satisfied, it seemed like a good compromise.

But if you're wondering what happens to all the extra fudgedog halves, Mrs. Podsner created a whole new food type for the second time in six months. And that's gotta be some kind of a record.

<u>Friday</u>

One of the reasons kids at my school don't take their education seriously enough is because we don't have a lot of good role models.

The most famous person to come out of our school is Larry Mack, and he went to prison. And the SECOND most famous person is his son, Larry Mack Junior, who dropped out to take over the family business when his dad got put away.

But I don't think Larry Mack Junior has any regrets about not finishing his education, because from his ads he seems to be doing just fine.

His family looks like it's doing all right, too. Larry Mack Junior has a bunch of kids, and he uses them in his television ads. And people can't get enough of his youngest son, Larry Mack Junior Junior.

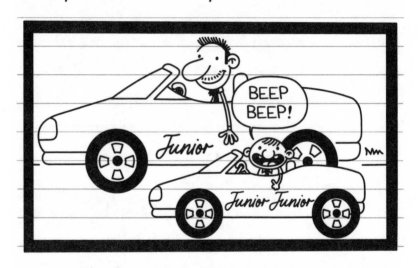

I actually feel a little bad for that kid, because with a name like that, his only choice in life is to take over the car dealership when his dad decides to hang it up. So anything he does between now and then doesn't really matter.

I think it's kind of crazy that your parents come up with your name before you're even born, and then you're stuck with it for the rest of your life.

It feels to me like you need to get to know a person before picking a name that fits them.

In some cultures, they wait a year before they decide on your permanent name. But that's still probably not enough time.

Because if my parents named me when I turned one, I would've ended up with a pretty terrible name.

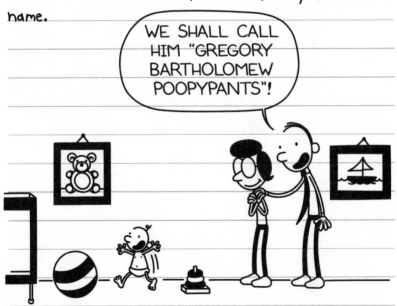

WE SHALL CALL HIM "GREGORY BARTHOLOMEW POOPYPANTS"!

Other cultures let kids come up with their OWN names once they're old enough. But I'm not sure that's such a great idea, either.

Because if you let kids my age name themselves, they'd probably just end up using their video game handles as their permanent names.

Harmlesspotato_196   SquiddyInkster   MoldyToez_1989

Some people legally change their names, but I don't see the point of going through all that hassle. Because I'll bet my family would just keep calling me by my old name anyway.

WOULD YOU LIKE SOME MORE GARLIC BREAD, GREG?

I TOLD YOU, IT'S "TECHNO LASERAXE"!

Sometimes I wonder if I'd be a completely different person if I was just named something a little cooler.

But maybe your name has nothing to do with the person you turn into. Because there's a girl at my school whose first name is Angel, and that doesn't seem to have made any difference in her case.

Back in olden times, your last name was just whatever you did for a living. And even though that made things simple, it must've made it really hard if you wanted to switch jobs.

Nowadays, you can be whatever you want to be, and I've got big plans for how I'm gonna make a name for myself.

But if I ever do get famous, I'm gonna be real careful about how my name gets used. Because the last thing you want is to have your name on something that hurts your reputation.

GREG HEFFLEY SEWAGE TREATMENT FACILITY

CLAP CLAP

CLAP CLAP

If I was Larry Mack Junior, I wouldn't want my family name on one of the worst-performing middle schools in the state, because that definitely can't be good for their car dealerships.

The crazy thing is, if Larry Mack Junior would just return some of the money his dad took from our school, it could help us turn things around.

But ever since his family moved out of town a long time ago, Larry Mack Junior probably hasn't given a second thought to the middle school named after his father.

Last summer, the state decided to build a new baseball stadium, and to pay for it they had to take money away from the fire department, the library, and the schools. And people were protesting outside the stadium over the budget cuts.

The worst thing is that since our school did so bad on the standardized test, we got the most money taken away. So now I guess we're supposed to do more with less.

Principal Bottoms has made all sorts of new rules to help the school save money, starting with capping the amount of materials each kid is allowed to use per week.

It used to be that if you wanted to use the stapler or a couple of paper clips, you just took what you needed off the teacher's desk. But now each kid gets nineteen staples and six paper clips a quarter, plus four glue-stick swipes.

	Staples	Paper clips	Glue-stick swipes
J. Healy	19	6	4
G. Heffley	19	6	4
A. Hendricks	19	6	4

If you need more than that, you've gotta bring your own supplies from home. And Ricky Fisher's been taking advantage of the situation because his mom works at the local office supply store and gets stuff at a discount.

The students aren't the only ones who get less materials to work with. Each teacher only gets one dry-erase marker per week, so they have to make it last. And sometimes I feel like my History teacher skims over important stuff just to save marker fluid.

WORLD HISTORY

When something breaks in a classroom, they don't even bother to fix it anymore. Last week, the handle on the pencil sharpener broke off in Geometry, and everyone had to gnaw their pencils to a point so they could take the quiz.

Lately, people have started handing Ruby Bird their pencils to ask HER to sharpen them. And I'm still not exactly sure how that works.

But classroom supplies are just the tip of the iceberg, because the school is taking all sorts of steps to make its pennies go further.

Earlier this week, the school started cutting off the heat after lunch. And by the time sixth period rolls around, you'd better hope you remembered to grab your coat out of your locker.

The one class that's not freezing is Science, and that's because we've been firing up the Bunsen burners to keep warm. But I'm a little nervous because we only have enough propane to last another week or two.

The school's been scrimping on electricity, too. To save money, they shut off the overhead lights in the C wing, and you can tell which kids have their lockers in that section of the school because they're the ones who walk into homeroom with dilated pupils.

The only kid who doesn't seem to mind that the lights are off in the C wing is Evelyn Trimble, but everybody says she might actually be a vampire.

Another way the school decided to save some money was by canceling their contract with the exterminator. So now, on top of everything else, we've gotta deal with cockroaches that are so big you can hear them when they walk in the room.

STEP
STEP
STEP

At first, whenever a kid spotted a cockroach, they stepped on it. But the teachers hated that because it was cruel, and it also left a mess.

So the new rule is that if you see a bug on the floor you have to put a cup over it. And in some classes we've had half a dozen cups scooting around at once.

DROP

Usually, one of the janitors collects all the cups at the end of the day and sets the bugs free outside. But I guess on Wednesday the janitor in charge of collecting the cups was out sick, so the night cleaning crew got a nasty surprise.

Roaches aren't the only insect we've got issues with, though. Some honeybees got into one of the classrooms in the C wing, and eventually the school just decided to let them keep it.

The insects are annoying, but if you ask me, the RODENTS are the real problem. Ever since the school canceled the exterminator, mice have been getting into the lockers and going through our lunch bags.

It's gotten so bad that the school had to make a rule that everyone who brings lunch to school has to keep it in the front office. But you end up spending half the lunch period just trying to figure out which brown paper bag is yours.

SNIFF
SNIFF

What's worse is that kids who have lunch in the earlier periods have started raiding our lunch bags and taking our snacks. And sometimes they'll swap something that they don't want from THEIR bag, which is how I ended up with a pickle instead of a chocolate chip cookie.

I got tired of people stealing my lunch snack, so I decided to do something about it. This week I started bringing Manny's lunch box to school, which has a lock on it.

A couple of kids who have lunch right before us got curious about what was in my lunch box and tried to bust it open. But I guess those metal boxes are built to withstand a real beating, because they couldn't crack it open no matter how hard they tried.

WHAM

It didn't really matter anyway. My snack for that day was a bag of sour cream and onion potato chips, but by the time I opened it the chips had turned to dust.

I kind of wish the school would just cough up the money for an exterminator, because trying to take care of the problem themselves has created a pretty dangerous situation.

The school set out mousetraps all over the building, so now you've gotta be real careful about where you put your hands, especially in the library.

I guess the school is just trying to save money wherever they can. And the latest place they're cutting back on is assemblies.

Our school used to go all out on assemblies. Last fall, we had three different authors come to our school, plus the illustrator of Commando Crocodile.

A few weeks after that, a zookeeper brought in a bunch of exotic animals, like penguins and an alligator that was ten feet long.

In February, we had an assembly where a scientist in a white lab coat and goggles did all sorts of cool experiments onstage. And even though it seemed a little dangerous, it was still pretty cool.

But I guess the school doesn't have money for that type of thing anymore, and now our assemblies aren't anything to get excited about.

Last week, we had an assembly called "Living Presidents," where each president gave a speech about their time in office. But one actor did all the parts, and I'm pretty sure it was the same guy who played Clarence Cluster.

And they probably shouldn't have let him have lunch in the cafeteria afterward, because if you ask me, it kind of broke the spell.

TWO FUDGEDOG FINGERS, PLEASE!

On Tuesday, we had an assembly that caused a big stir for all the wrong reasons. Randy from Randy's Reptile Revue accidentally let one of his snakes get loose, which caused a total panic in the gym.

The good news is that the snake was spotted in the hallway the next day. But I don't think anyone's gonna tell Randy, because that thing is single-handedly taking care of our rodent problem.

Thursday

This money situation at school is getting pretty serious, and now teachers are starting to leave.

Apparently, the whole teaching staff was supposed to get a raise this spring. But when Principal Bottoms told them it wasn't gonna happen, a few of them actually quit on the spot.

That meant that all of a sudden I didn't have a History teacher. So the school put Leonard Burry in charge of teaching, since he's been held back twice and this is his third time taking the class.

Mr. Frum quit, too, which means now Mrs. Lackey is the only Social Studies teacher in our grade. So they actually removed the wall between two classrooms and now Mrs. Lackey can teach twice as many kids at once.

But even after some teachers left on their own, the school made more cuts to the staff. They switched Ms. Masie from full-time to three days a week, and they let one of the school nurses go, so now we're down to just one.

The new rule is that you're only allowed to go to the nurse's office if it's for something urgent, like a medical emergency. And each classroom has a sign next to the door to see if your situation qualifies.

STOP!

Do you really need to see the school nurse?

Please stay in class if you have a:

☐ runny nose   ☐ blister
☐ hangnail   ☐ pimple
☐ paper cut   ☐ hiccups

Personally, I think the new policy is reasonable, because I'm pretty sure that some kids were going to the nurse's office just to get out of class.

Other kids were using the nurse as a free psychologist. I heard David Sneed used to visit the nurse's office to talk about his fear of underground supervolcanoes.

Now every teacher has to take care of minor medical issues in the classroom, which is taking a lot of time away from doing their actual jobs. Yesterday, Ms. Pritchard spent the whole period putting bandages on kids who got injured making paper airplanes when she stepped out of the room.

But teachers aren't doctors, and I don't love the idea of someone who's not qualified giving me medical treatment. So when I got a splinter in my butt from doing sit-ups on the gym floor, I decided I'd just wait until I got home to take care of it myself.

The people who got hit the hardest by all these budget cuts were the janitorial staff, whose team went down from ten to three. And the worst part is that the janitors who lost their jobs got replaced by a machine that cleans the floors.

The school bought a secondhand robot from a local grocery store. At first, some kids were uncomfortable being around a faceless machine, so the school put googly eyes on it to make it seem a little more human. But if you ask me, that makes it even creepier.

WHIRRR

And I don't know if it's such a great idea to have a machine cleaning up after everyone. Because now people just throw their trash on the floor since they know the robot will pick it up.

TOSS

It's not only the students, either. Teachers have been taking full advantage of having a cleaning robot in the school, and I'm pretty sure Mrs. Lackey has been bringing trash from home.

SHAKE
SHAKE

I also think it was a mistake giving the robot eyes, because now it thinks it's a person. Lately, it's been skipping out on its job and going to class with all the other students. And yesterday, I'm pretty sure it was copying off my quiz in Science.

I just hope this thing doesn't get TOO smart, though. Because it really wouldn't be good if machines started taking everyone's jobs.

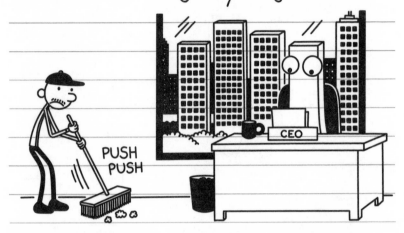

The robot's not the only one the school's getting free labor out of, though. They got the local prison to make furniture for our classrooms. And I'm not trying to complain or anything, but the rear legs on my chair in Social Studies are a good six inches shorter than the front ones.

Some of the inmates write their names on the furniture they make. And a guy named Justin carved a note on my desk that makes me sad every time I read it.

Sometimes they'll even draw pictures on the furniture. And someone sketched out a whole escape plan on the front of Mr. Rask's desk, which the school had to paint over.

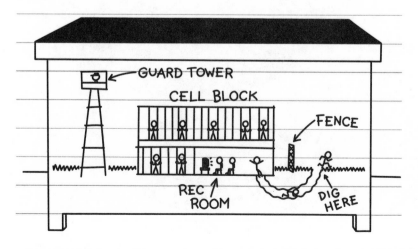

<u>Wednesday</u>

It turns out the steps the school's been taking to save money haven't been enough, because now they're looking for ways to MAKE money. And Principal Bottoms's first idea was the Platinum High Flyers Club.

The Platinum level is like the regular High Flyers Club, but the big difference is that you don't have to get good grades to be a member. You just need to be willing to fork over $12.99 a month.

Or you need to have PARENTS who are willing to pay the membership fee. And Stephen Birch is lucky his folks make a ton of money in their construction business, because with his grades he had no chance of earning his way in.

I tried to convince MY parents to sign me up for the Platinum level, but when my mom said I could join if I'd be willing to give up my monthly video game membership, I decided to drop the whole idea.

I'm starting to rethink that decision, though, because the perks in the Platinum level are way better than the free version, starting with the premium seating.

Principal Bottoms has a brother who owns a used furniture store, and he sold a bunch of leather recliners to the school at a steep discount.

Those things tilt all the way back to a lie-flat position, which makes things pretty uncomfortable for the people who sit behind them, especially during tests.

The kids in the Platinum level also get premium snacks, like popcorn and full-size candy bars.

So I'll bet the regular High Flyers feel dopey about their tiny bags of peanuts now.

The Platinum High Flyers don't even have to be in the classroom if they don't want to be. They each get a special Platinum Pass, which lets them go wherever they want whenever they want.

Plus, they can use their Platinum Passes for all sorts of different things, like skipping the line at lunch, which is kind of annoying for everyone else.

They even get their own seating section in the cafeteria, with tablecloths and real silverware instead of plastic utensils. And this week, they introduced table service to the Platinum seating section, so those kids don't even have to get up if they want a refill on their drinks.

RESERVED
FOR
PLATINUM
DINERS

The Platinum High Flyers Club is causing some serious resentment from the teachers, too.

The Platinum kids complain a lot more than everyone else, and yesterday one of my classes got held up for twenty minutes after Marlene Cindrich made a big stink about the view from her window seat.

On top of that, the Platinum kids are always either too hot or too cold, and now the teachers have to keep fresh blankets in the classrooms.

FLOOF

The thing the teachers are the maddest about is that with all the new members to the High Flyers Club, the teachers' lounge is always full of kids. So now the teachers have to use the janitors' closet when they take their breaks.

But the Platinum High Flyers Club isn't the only way the school is trying to make money. They're also selling corporate sponsorships.

That's where a company pays a bunch of cash to put their logo somewhere in the school. Ever since Principal Bottoms gave the green light for these kinds of deals, there are ads everywhere you look.

When you walk through one of the hallways in our school, you feel like you're in the middle of Times Square.

There are ads on all the surfaces, including the water fountains, which some soda company paid a lot of money to sponsor.

There are even ads on the FLOORS. And ever since Triple-Decker Treats started putting stickers in the hallways, kids have been leaving school early to go get ice cream.

I don't think there's a place they WON'T put an ad. The latest place they've put them is inside our lockers.

Bull's-Eye Grocery even paid to put stickers
in the urinals, and I'm actually glad they did,
because now the floors in the boys' bathroom are a
lot less sticky.

Companies that are willing to pay more can sponsor
whole ROOMS, which is why our English classroom
is now the Davidson's Dictionary Center, and
Social Studies became the Island Getaways Travel
Company Hub.

The computer lab is sponsored by a company that makes video games, and they went kind of crazy with their branding.

Now Entering the

Murlak's Gate

Computer Center

They donated new computers with one of their most popular games preloaded, so now the school can forget about kids getting any work done in there.

CRUNCH CHOP

Speaking of donations, a company that makes luxury pajamas sponsored the teachers' lounge and stocked it with robes and slippers. So the kids in the High Flyers Club don't even bother going to class anymore.

But you don't have to spend a fortune to get an ad in our school, because they're offering a ton of smaller sponsorship opportunities, too. Even our staplers have ads on them now.

I'm not sure every one of these sponsorships is a good idea, though. Some magazine paid to put a sample of their publication inside our Science textbooks, and it feels to me like the school should be a little more choosy about who they take their money from.

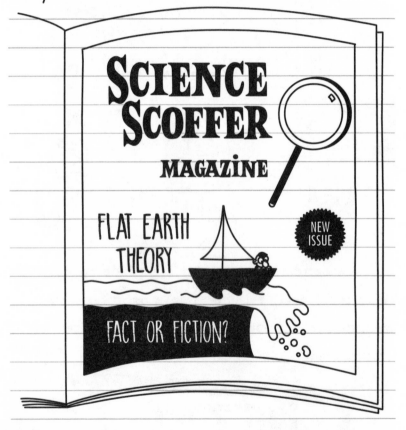

A few companies even signed exclusive deals to get their products into the school.

So now all the vending machines are stocked with snacks from a company that makes spicy potato chips.

I guess Blisterin' Hot Chips paid a lot of money to be the exclusive salty snack supplier, and as part of the deal nobody's allowed to have chips from another company on school property. So if someone catches you with a different brand, they'll make sure you don't get to enjoy them.

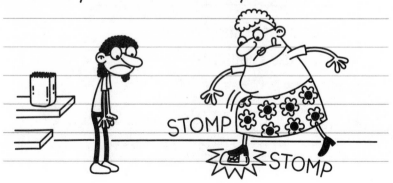

They also get product placement in the morning news program the school streams into all the classrooms. And I kind of feel bad for the student reporters who have to pretend to like it.

It's not only the morning program, either. Blisterin' Hot Chips sponsors the school newspaper, and these days it's hard to tell what's an ad and what's actual news.

The Student Crier

Blisterin' Hot Chips Proven to Increase Popularity

In a new study, Blisterin' Hot Chips consumption is closely tied to middle-school popularity ranking, with a positive correlation between the number of bags consumed and a student's favorability with their peers.

Unpopular no more: Former loser Thomas Mayfew is now riding high

It feels like there's no limit to what the school's willing to sell. Some plumbing company just bought the rights to the gymnasium, and there's apparently all sorts of stuff that comes with that.

Their logo is in the middle of the gym floor and on the clothes we have to wear for Phys Ed. The plumbing company even replaced Fudgy with their own mascot, which hasn't been super popular with the students.

"FLUSHY"

All these sponsorships are small potatoes compared to the one thing the school's been holding out on, which is naming rights for the school itself. They think there's a company that might be willing to pay big bucks to put their name on our building.

They even put an ad in the local paper to try and find a bidder.

YOUR NAME HERE!

Rename Our Middle School!
Imagine your company's name emblazoned on our building in two-foot-tall lettering!
Call Principal Bottoms today!

But I guess there aren't a lot of companies willing to be connected with a school that doesn't have the best reputation, because after getting zero takers, Principal Bottoms had to lower the asking price.

Eventually, someone put in a bid to rename our school. But it wasn't a company, it was a TOWN.

It came from Slacksville, which we share a border with. And we've been at war with those guys for YEARS.

They're still mad at us for getting the state to put a garbage dump on their side of the town line. So they tried to get their revenge by putting a wind turbine in the middle of the dump to blow the garbage smell back at US. But it turns out wind turbines don't act like giant fans, so they totally wasted their money on that one.

We decided to really stick it to Slacksville by putting up a billboard right on the border between our two towns. And apparently their property values went down by 30% after that.

At least we don't live in *Slacksville!*

So Slacksville's plan to get us back is to rename our middle school. But even though they were willing to pay, Principal Bottoms decided to reject it anyway.

LARRY MACK MIDDLE SCHOOL

Name Change Form

Proposed name:

Slacksville Rules! Middle School

The school decided to lower the asking price AGAIN and finally found a taker, which was the exterminator whose contract the school canceled a couple of weeks back.

The president of the company even came to the school to make the offer in person.

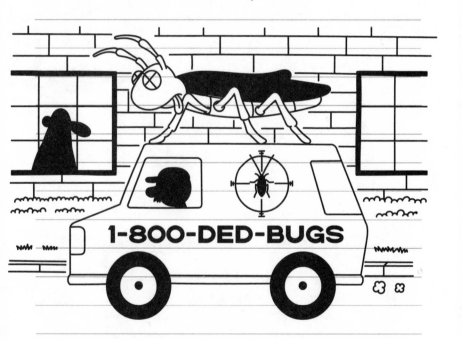

1-800-DED-BUGS

And even though no one's thrilled our new name is gonna be 1-800-DED-BUGS Middle School, everyone seems to agree that it's still better than the name Slacksville came up with.

The exterminator and the school put on a big press conference to announce the deal, and all the local stations came out to cover it.

But the exterminator probably should've waited until AFTER his company got rid of the pests in the school. Because I doubt that press conference was good for his business.

<u>Friday</u>

Apparently, a lot of parents aren't thrilled with the new name of the school, and they don't like all the advertising we're being exposed to, either. So they let Principal Bottoms know about it at a PTA meeting.

Now Principal Bottoms has a new scheme to raise money, and it's already created some pretty big changes at school.

The school figured they could get a lot of money by renting out classrooms to people who needed space. So now the C wing is full of grown-ups who are using the classrooms for all sorts of different things.

Some of them rented classrooms for extra storage, and now they're filled with boxes that people couldn't fit in their garages.

A few others have set up rooms to do remote work so they don't have to drive into the city every day. And some are even using the rooms to create their own businesses.

One of my neighbors, Mrs. Jackson, started renting our Home Ec room, and she's using the ovens to run a bakery. Now there's a line around the block for her blueberry muffins every morning.

Unfortunately, my Science classroom is across the courtyard from the C-wing classrooms, and sometimes the smell of whatever she's baking is a little too much. Today she made snickerdoodles smack in the middle of a pop quiz, and it drove everybody in my class totally wild.

SNIFFFF

PANT, PANT!

Speaking of distractions, someone turned one of the rooms into a hot yoga studio, and my mom attends the class. But no kid wants to see their own mother in yoga pants, especially in the middle of a school day.

It's not just the smells and the sights that are causing problems. It's the SOUNDS, too.

There's a rock band of middle-aged guys who practice every day in one of the C-wing classrooms, and they're really awful. Then there's the constant barking that echoes through the heating vents all day long.

At first I thought someone was using a room to run a kennel or something, but it's actually the police department, who's using our old Art room to train attack dogs.

The only good news is that one renter managed to take back control of the room that all the honeybees took over, and now she sells beeswax candles and lip balm at the mall.

I guess I'm glad that the school figured out a new way to make money, but it's bad news for us students. All our classes got packed into the other two wings, so things are more crowded than ever.

Plus, now we have to share the cafeteria with the renters, which can be a little awkward.

The school's not just renting out our classrooms, though. On Thursday nights they rent the gym to the high school for basketball games.

But whenever there's a game, the fans completely trash our gym, and we have to clean up their mess the next day.

Even though there's a policy against having food in the gym, the people who go to those high-school games don't care. So there's always a ton of potato chip bags and half-eaten hot dogs under the bleachers.

Some kids actually scavenge for leftover snacks and resell them in the cafeteria. And believe it or not, people will pay good money for food that's been on the floor.

pretzels corn chips mix 'n' match
candy raisins

The school rents out the gym on weekends, too. And the reason I know that is because my church has been using the space while the pews are getting replaced.

But it doesn't seem right to have religious services in a place where we have Phys Ed during the week. Because the whole time, all I can think about is everything ELSE that's happened in that gym.

Saturday

Every year the parents in the PTA put on an auction to raise money for the school, but this year they wanted to make it bigger than ever to earn as much as possible.

They asked students to volunteer to help at the event. And since my mom is the secretary of the PTA, I got roped into going.

The PTA auction is a pretty fancy affair, so I had to dress up for it. And my job was to walk around with a tray stacked with miniature pigs in a blanket all night.

To be honest, it was a little awkward being around my parents when they were having fun with their friends. But I guess people my mom and dad's age don't get a lot of chances to go out, so they were probably just happy for the opportunity to cut loose.

There were two parts to the night. The first part was the silent auction, where there are different prizes and gift baskets you can win by being the highest bidder.

And the way you do that is by writing down how much money you're willing to pay.

I was hoping my parents would bid on something cool, like a week at a ski condo during winter vacation, or a pair of Jet Skis.

But the only item my mom put her name on was a wellness basket, and since she was the only bidder, she won.

A bunch of local companies donated some quality items for the silent auction. East Bay Barbeque supplied a brand-new outdoor grill, and the Scouts kicked in a s'mores kit with a half dozen mugs for hot chocolate.

But a few companies seemed to be just trying to unload stuff they couldn't use.

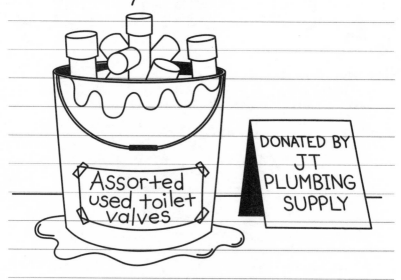

I'm pretty sure some companies donate every year because Crawford Studios offered a family portrait, which is what they did for the last PTA auction. And the reason I know that is because last year my family actually WON it.

When Mom told us we were doing a family portrait, I was a little annoyed because it meant I had to dress up on a Saturday. But it was actually a lot worse than that.

I thought we were gonna take a quick picture and I could enjoy the rest of my weekend. But it was a PAINTING, which meant we had to go back five times.

Halfway through the first session, Manny wouldn't sit still anymore, and the artist kept having to start that part of the painting over. But Rodrick was even worse, because he didn't go back for the rest of the sessions.

So the artist had to paint Rodrick from memory, which is why the painting is in our basement and not above the fireplace in the family room.

I didn't want a repeat of THAT nightmare, which is why this year I wrote a made-up name on the bidding sheet to make sure there was no chance our family actually won it.

FAMILY PORTRAIT

1. Taylor — $50
2. Richardson — $75
3. Bergonhoff — $8,000

The next part of the night was the live auction, where they hired a professional auctioneer to get people to bid on a bunch of special prizes. And since parents were all trying to outbid each other by raising their paddles, it actually got pretty wild.

The first prize in the live auction was a chance for your kid to ride to school in a fire truck. Everyone seemed pretty excited about that one, and people started driving up the bids right from the start.

I'm surprised they still offer that prize after what happened last year, though.

Lily Stubman's parents outbid everyone else, so their daughter got to ride the fire truck to school. And I guess it was fun for a little while.

But on the way there an actual fire broke out at some restaurant downtown, and the firefighters had to race to the building to deal with it. So Lily Stubman ended up on the news, and I'm pretty sure she's still scarred by the whole experience.

The next item up for auction was just like the
fire-truck thing, only with a police squad car.
Ricky Fisher's parents won it for the second year
in a row, so I guess they figure it's good practice
for him later on in life.

The next item was Lunch with the Librarian, and
Ms. Masie fetched a lot of money since she's so
popular with the kids.

But they probably shouldn't have put Lunch with a Janitor next, because the guy they picked for it always yells at us when we step on his clean floors.

Nobody was willing to raise their paddle to start the bidding, and it was pretty uncomfortable for a while there. But eventually Mr. Gupta offered three bucks just to move things along.

After that was over, the auctioneer announced the next prize, which was to have a teacher come to your house to do odd jobs.

I'm surprised teachers agreed to that one, because I'll bet the last place they want to be on the weekend is at some family's house fixing their mailbox or whatever.

But that's exactly what happened when my parents won that auction item one year.

It's hard for me to imagine teachers having lives of their own, so it's always a little weird when you see them outside the school environment.

It always takes me a little off guard, especially when it happens in places you're not expecting it.

The next prize was one they've been doing for years, which is to raise money to get the principal to kiss a piglet. Principal Mancy used to do it at a big assembly, and kids would go absolutely nuts.

The auctioneer got things going, and parents started driving the bidding up. But Principal Bottoms walked onstage to say he couldn't do it because he's allergic to "barn animals."

So either he's telling the truth or he's just not the kind of person who's into kissing pigs.

People moved on pretty quick, because everyone was excited about the last live auction item, which was Principal for the Day. That's where a kid gets to sit in the principal's office and do the morning announcements and pretend they're in charge for a few hours.

It's kind of a dumb prize if you ask me, since the winner doesn't actually get any real power. But I guess every parent wants their kid to feel special, so as soon as the auctioneer started the bidding, things got a little crazy.

I noticed my mom put her paddle up. At first I thought she was just trying to encourage other people to raise their bids and get the price up, but then I realized she was actually trying to WIN.

The price kept climbing higher and higher, and people started dropping out. But every time someone raised their paddle, Mom raised HERS. And even though Dad tried to stop her, Mom was locked in.

It finally came down to the last two people, Mom and Mrs. O'Malley, and there's some history between those two.

They ran against each other to be PTA secretary, and after Mom won, Mrs. O'Malley accused her of spreading rumors to steal the election, which Mom denied. So this bidding war was PERSONAL for them. And it didn't help that the crowd was egging them both on.

I don't think Mom or Mrs. O'Malley actually cared about the Principal for the Day thing anymore. They both just wanted to make sure the OTHER person didn't win it.

Eventually, Mrs. O'Malley came to her senses and dropped out of the running, which meant Mom was the top bidder. And from the way she reacted, you'd think she won the lottery.

I don't know how much the final bid was, and to be honest, I don't even WANT to know. But I have a feeling there are going to be a lot fewer Christmas presents under the tree this year.

<u>Monday</u>

This morning, I begged Mom not to make me go to school. But she said the Principal for the Day thing cost her a fortune, and she wanted to get her money's worth. She even made me wear a shirt and tie so I'd look "official."

I went to school and reported directly to the front office. I figured Principal Bottoms would have me do the morning announcements and maybe tag along with him for a few hours. But when I got to his office he seemed annoyed that I was a few minutes late.

Principal Bottoms handed me a name tag and a set of keys that he said could get me into any room in the building.

Then he wished me luck and took off, which meant I was on my own.

So I had the principal's office all to myself, which was actually pretty sweet. And I thought that if this is what it feels like to be in charge, I could definitely get used to it.

But the moment didn't last long. Because three minutes after the bell rang, the school secretary came in with a pile of papers and told me I needed to go through the day's mail.

It was all bills and repair estimates and a bunch of boring stuff I didn't even understand. But before I was halfway through opening the envelopes, the school secretary brought me some checks she said I needed to sign.

I don't even know if it's actually legal for a kid my age to sign a check, but I figured these people probably needed to get paid, so I scribbled my name down on each one.

DATE __May 8__

PAY TO THE
ORDER OF __Cryan Landscaping__ $ | 1,248.00 |

__one thousand two hundred forty-eight dollars__

Greg Heffley

MEMO __mulch__

In the middle of signing checks, I got interrupted AGAIN. This time the secretary said there was a problem in the boys' bathroom in the B wing that I needed to deal with.

Some idiot had ripped a sink off the wall, and I'd be willing to bet it was Marty Vinson. So now a pipe was busted and it was flooding the bathroom with water.

I went to find a janitor to handle the problem, but they said plumbing repair wasn't in their contract, so there was nothing they could do about it.

By now things were really getting out of hand with the flooding situation, because there was water in the B-wing hallway. A bunch of kids had grabbed lunch trays from the cafeteria and were totally going nuts.

I knew it would take forever to get the plumbers out to the school, so I went back to the janitors to try and strike a deal.

I told them that if they fixed the leak in the bathroom, I'd give them this Friday off. But I guess those guys could tell they had me over a barrel, so they pushed for even more.

The janitors came up with a whole list of demands, like better dental care, longer breaks, and the chance to work remotely on Mondays and Wednesdays.

Even though I didn't know if I technically had the authority to agree to all that stuff, I figured if I didn't then the whole B wing would be under water before the end of the day.

SHAKE
SHAKE

After that situation was under control, I wanted to just go back to my office and take it easy until lunch.

But when I got there I was in for a surprise, because there were a bunch of kids waiting outside my door.

They were a few of the biggest troublemakers
in my grade. Their teachers sent them to the
principal's office, which meant that now I had to
deal with them.

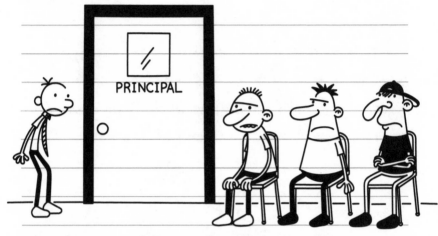

The thing is, I knew I couldn't come down too
hard on these kids because I was gonna have
to face them the next day when I WASN'T
principal. So I gave each of them a pep talk and
told them to try and make better choices.

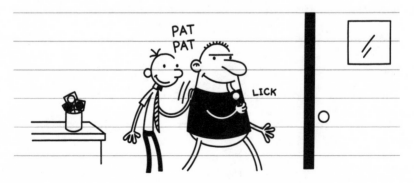

I made sure to send each one away with a lollipop to stay on their good side, but that turned out to be a big mistake. Because once word got back to the rest of the students that the principal was handing out candy for being bad, it caused a big stir.

All of a sudden kids were acting out in class to get sent to the principal's office. And it wasn't just the regular troublemakers, either.

In fact, one of them was Alex Aruda, who's the smartest kid in my grade. And a big fan of lollipops, apparently.

After I finally got finished dealing with the bad kids, I had to deal with the GOOD ones. And since this was the first time any of them had ever been sent to the principal's office, they seemed a little stressed out to be there.

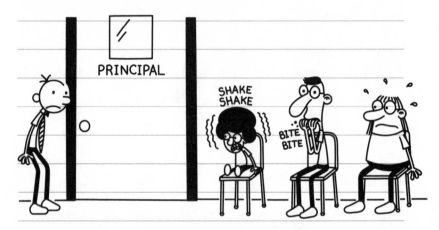

I didn't have time to deal with all these people, though, because the secretary told me I was already late for the weekly staff meeting in the conference room.

When I got there, I could tell from the looks on everyone's faces that this wasn't going to be a lot of fun. And I was right about that.

As soon as I sat down, the teachers launched into their complaints, which covered everything from how many dry-erase markers each one of them gets to the High Flyers Club kids using their lounge.

Before long, everyone was talking at once and I couldn't even make out what anyone was saying.

So I came up with a rule. I grabbed a stapler and told the teachers that if someone wanted to talk, then they had to be holding the stapler. And that worked for a little while.

Mrs. Lackey griped about how teachers should get to park their cars closer to the building, which seemed pretty reasonable to me.

But she kind of went on and on, and I realized we should probably create a time limit for how long you're allowed to hold the stapler.

Before I could announce the new rule, Mr. Ball snatched the stapler from Mrs. Lackey so he could talk about HIS issues.

And since he's six foot seven, there wasn't a lot anyone could do about it.

It turns out Mrs. O'Harris keeps a miniature stapler in her purse, so she whipped it out and started complaining that teachers should get free milk in the cafeteria. Even though everyone seemed to agree with her, nobody liked the fact that she was breaking the rules by using an unofficial stapler.

People started grabbing at it, and somehow Mr. Tupa ended up with the miniature stapler attached to his ear. We had to pause the meeting so he could go to the nurse's office and have it looked at.

I decided the stapler idea wasn't working, so I tried a different approach. The new deal was that if you wanted to talk, you had to raise your hand and wait to be acknowledged, which was a rule all the teachers seemed to understand.

I called on Mrs. Shelburn first, who has a beef with Ms. Pritchard over a computer.

The school bought a new laptop to replace a broken one, and they gave it to Ms. Pritchard. But Mrs. Shelburn thought that since she's been at the school longer, she deserved the new laptop.

The two of them started going at it in front of everybody, and they actually had to be separated.

I thought they each had a pretty valid claim to the new computer, but I couldn't think of a solution that would make them both happy.

Then I remembered a story from Sunday school about this wise king who had to deal with this exact same kind of thing.

I told the two teachers that they could split the laptop down the middle and each get half. I figured one of them would just let the other have the computer, because half a laptop is no good to anyone.

But I guess I underestimated how much these two teachers didn't want the other one to have the new laptop, because they split it right down the middle, and each took a half.

RIPPP

By the end of the meeting, I REALLY needed a break, but I wasn't off the hook yet.

A few of the C-wing renters were waiting outside my office, and I couldn't even imagine what this was going to be about.

Apparently, the police dogs got into a batch of Mrs. Jackson's oatmeal raisin cookies, so she wanted the police department to pay for her lost profits.

But the police said Mrs. Jackson was negligent for leaving the door to her classroom unlocked, and since raisins are toxic to dogs, they wanted her to pay their veterinarian bills. And I didn't even know where to start with THAT one.

Luckily, I didn't have to deal with it right then, because Vice Principal Roy came on the loudspeaker and said everyone needed to come down to the gym for a special assembly.

I had no idea what the assembly was about, but I honestly didn't care as long as I didn't have to actually do anything. But it turns out I was wrong about that.

When I saw the gym stage, I realized why Principal Bottoms was so eager to leave school today.

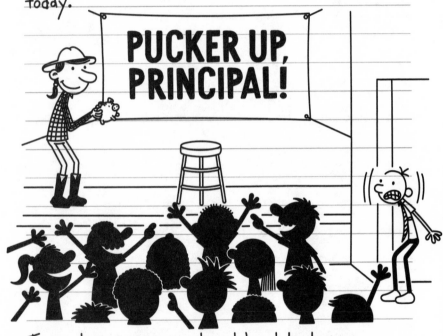

I tried to turn around and head back to my office, but there was already a wall of students blocking my way. So I knew there was no getting out of it.

And if you were ever curious about what it's like to kiss a pig, it's actually not as bad as you'd think.

I'm sure I had a few more hours on the clock, but by then I'd pretty much had my fill of being in charge.

So I left a note on the school secretary's desk and gave myself permission to leave a little early.

FROM THE PRINCIPAL'S DESK
———————————

I quit.

Tuesday

After being Principal for the Day, I was pretty
happy to just go back to being a regular student
for the rest of the year. But when I got to
school this morning, I found out that things are
about to change for EVERYONE.

The student paper comes out on Tuesdays, and
even though it's free, I don't usually bother
grabbing a copy. But this time I could tell they
had broken a big story.

According to the front page, the state is planning on closing the school. And the only way it can stay open is if we bring our scores up on the standardized test next week.

But based on the way things have been going this year, it doesn't seem like there's any chance of THAT happening.

I know this news is a big deal and all, but our student paper is always super dramatic with their headlines, and this time wasn't any different.

The Student Crier

THE END IS NEAR

Middle School to Close If Scores Don't Improve

Apparently, Principal Bottoms actually knew about this for a while, but I guess he didn't want to cause a panic right before we took the standardized test. The only reason the student paper found out about it at all is because they had a spy in the front office.

This reporter named Freddie Larkin had been faking injuries for the past two weeks so he could go to the nurse's office, which is right outside the conference room. And somehow, nobody caught on to what he was up to.

But the school probably should've broken the news themselves, because now everyone's in a panic. And nobody knows what's going to happen to us if the school DOES close.

The article said that if the state shuts us down, they're gonna split everyone up and send us to two different schools in neighboring towns.

One of the schools is Fulson Tech, which just opened last year and is supposedly really nice. In fact, I've heard some crazy things about HOW nice it is. Albert Sandy says their lunch menu was created by some famous chef, and they've even got a meat-carving station in the cafeteria.

They also have a massage therapist on staff to help kids reduce their stress, and a room with napping pods for when students need a break.

Their assemblies are pretty top-shelf, too. In the last year they had a Formula One driver and a team of astronauts who are headed to Mars, which kind of makes Randy's Reptile Revue seem a little cheesy by comparison.

So if you end up getting sent to Fulson Tech, you're all set. It's the OTHER place everyone's worried about, which is Slacksville Middle School.

Slacksville's building is older than ours, and it doesn't have air-conditioning. They can't even open their windows to get some fresh air when the weather's warm because the middle school is right next to the state dump.

It's not just the students who are worried about what's going to happen to them. It's the teachers, too. They know that if the school closes, they could lose their jobs.

So at this point, Ms. Pritchard has given up on teaching Geometry completely because she's trying to plan for her future.

The rest of the staff has started looking, too. Our newest janitor even posted something on the bulletin board to see if he can get work if this whole thing blows up.

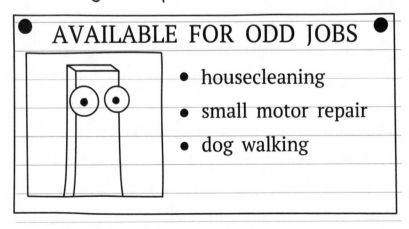

<u>Thursday</u>

I got some seriously good news yesterday. The student paper found out which kids are going where if the school closes, and they posted the list on the bulletin board in the main entrance.

And I'm happy to say that if we get shut down, I'm headed to Fulson Tech.

I thought the way the school would split us up would be by sending kids whose last names started with A-M to one place and the kids whose last names started with N-Z to the other. But I guess they wanted to be fair, so they did it by alternating between names.

That's lucky for me, but not so lucky for Jenna Healy and Alfonso Hendricks.

> Healy, Jenna — Slacksville
>
> Heffley, Greg — Fulson Tech
>
> Hendricks, Alfonso — Slacksville

Unfortunately, Rowley's name didn't fall in the right spot, which means he'll be going to Slacksville. And even though I told him I'd bring home leftover prime rib from the Fulson Tech cafeteria every day, it didn't seem to cheer him up any.

Rowley's all stressed out, and so are half the other kids at my school. Their only hope at this point is that the school does well on the standardized test and the state doesn't shut us down.

A few kids' parents even hired private tutors to help them study, and Rowley's parents got him a different tutor for every single subject. And that stinks for me, because it means he doesn't have any free time to hang out after school.

I think Rowley's parents went a little overboard with this tutoring stuff, though. They even got him a Phys Ed tutor, and I'm pretty sure none of that stuff is gonna be on the test.

Things are changing faster at school than I can keep up with.

A few parents decided to just pull the plug and send their kids to private school instead. And I'm not gonna say I was sad to see Marty Vinson go.

Danny Tang's parents decided to pull him out, too, which meant I finally had a locker all to myself.

Then something happened that made a giant mess of things. Alex Aruda's parents decided they didn't feel like waiting, so they enrolled him in a boarding school on the other side of the state. But since he's got a name at the front of the alphabet, it had a ripple effect through the whole list.

Now every kid who was supposed to go to Slacksville is going to Fulson Tech, and every kid who was supposed to go to Fulson Tech is headed to Slacksville instead. And everyone found out when the student paper posted the new list on the bulletin board.

So things got flipped upside down, and all the kids in my group were totally thrown for a loop.

But everyone ELSE was on top of the world. And you'd think that kids like Jenna Healy and Alfonso Hendricks might be a little more considerate about celebrating around the rest of us.

A bunch of kids tried convincing this girl named Eva Aaronson to drop out and go to private school, because if she did, it would flip the list back to how it was.

But I guess she was really looking forward to those napping pods, because even after we offered her all our snacks, she wouldn't budge.

On the walk home from school, Rowley said he'd bring me his leftovers from the meat-carving station every day. And I know he was just trying to make me feel better, but for some reason it really got on my nerves.

I tried to get my parents to pull me out of school and send me to a school with perks like they have at Fulson Tech. But even after I went over all the benefits, they said private school was too expensive.

<u>Monday</u>

I figured the only chance I had of changing my situation was to do my best on that standardized test and hope everyone else did THEIR part. So this weekend, I hit the books.

The problem is, it's not easy catching up on a whole year of school. And I didn't even know where to start.

I tried to give myself little breaks every now and then to keep myself motivated. But I guess I got a little carried away, because I ended up spending more time reading romance novels than school textbooks.

I realized my strategy wasn't working, so I decided to try a totally different approach. I figured if I surrounded myself with my textbooks, I might be able to just absorb all the information into my brain somehow.

But I don't think it really worked, because when I woke up this morning I didn't feel any smarter.

On top of that, the ink they use to print those textbooks with must be really cheap, because I ended up with the periodic table of elements stuck to my cheek.

You can tell a lot of kids are really nervous about the test tomorrow, because they're doing all sorts of crazy things for good luck.

Some people have been bringing horseshoes and other good luck charms to school. And Ricky Fisher's been selling trinkets he swears will get your math score up by twenty points.

Some kids think that it's good luck if you only step on the red tiles on the school floors, but others say the red ones are BAD luck. And that's creating a dangerous situation in the hallways.

I feel especially bad for this kid everyone calls Lucky. The way I heard it, he almost got struck by lightning playing golf with his dad, which is how he got his nickname.

KZOCK

Everybody's saying if you rub Lucky's head, his luck will rub off on YOU. So everyone's been trying to get a piece of him. Now Lucky's got a bald spot, and I'm hoping for his sake it's not permanent.

Some people are so desperate to do well on this test that they've even turned to the statue of Larry Mack. They've been leaving candles and making offerings to his shoes in hopes that somehow it'll help.

But the school said it was a fire hazard, so today they cleared the stuff out.

FWOOSH

All I can say is that if we're counting on Larry Mack's feet to save us tomorrow, we could be in even more trouble than I thought.

<u>Tuesday</u>

Today was the day of the big standardized test, which was scheduled to start at 8:30 and be over at noon. And even though I did my best to prepare for it, I was still nervous because I've never been a great test-taker.

The problem is that I get distracted really easily. So if someone in the room is humming or chewing gum, it totally breaks my concentration. And since half the kids in my grade didn't even care how they did on this thing, there were way more distractions today than usual.

THWAP

I really wish I had thought ahead and brought some noise-canceling headphones or something to block out the sound. The only kid in the room who could actually focus was Lucky, who wore a helmet to stop people from rubbing his head.

I felt a little better knowing Lucky was trying to do well on the test, because he's pretty smart and I figured he'd get our test scores up. I also knew we couldn't count on Andrew Huck to be the one to come through for us.

But the bigger problem was with the kids who were headed to Fulson Tech, because I realized they weren't even gonna TRY to do well.

In fact, I suspected those kids were trying to do bad on PURPOSE. And when I peeked at Jenna Healy's answer sheet, that pretty much confirmed it.

I figured the only thing I could do was try my hardest and hope for the best. But the test itself was practically impossible, and it felt like whoever wrote the questions didn't actually want anyone to succeed.

Please fill in the choice that best answers the above question.

    A 1
    B 1 and 3
    C 1 and 2 but not 4
    D All of the above
    E None of the above

In the end, none of it mattered anyway. A half hour into the test, a bee flew into the room, which nobody seemed to notice except me.

But that one bee was followed by a whole SWARM
of bees a minute later, and we all had to evacuate
the classroom.

BZZZZZZZZZZZZZZZZ

It turns out the snake that escaped from the
assembly got into the room the police were renting
in the C wing, and totally freaked out the dogs.
So the dogs busted down their door to escape.

SLITHER

The beekeeper got curious about all the commotion in the hallway and cracked open her door, which was a huge mistake.

The bees got into our classrooms, and all the students had to wait in the parking lot while the fire department took care of the situation inside. And this was one of those times when it would've been really nice to have more than one school nurse.

Monday

Our school's standardized test scores came back, and let's just say the results weren't good. Nobody even got past the math section, and apparently the state doesn't give you a do-over if your classrooms get invaded by bees.

That means our school officially closed on Friday, and the student paper marked it with one last special edition. And even though I haven't had a ton of fun in this place, it still felt like a sad day.

The Student Crier

IT'S OVER

Middle School to Close Its Doors for Good

Not everybody was broken up about the school closing, though. The kids who were going to Fulson Tech seemed pretty jazzed, and Mrs. Lackey was excited to head off on a cruise with her husband.

But the person who seemed the MOST excited was Principal Bottoms. And now that I think of it, he's probably been checked out for a while.

Today was the start of my new life as a Slacksville Middle School student. But if every day is going to be like this one, I could be in for a rough ride.

First of all, I had to get up a whole hour earlier to catch the bus, which meant it was still kind of dark. And it's a little depressing being at the bus stop when the moon is still out.

But it got worse from there. Since I'm the only kid in my neighborhood who's going to Slacksville, they can't put me on a regular bus. That meant they had to send someone to pick me up for school.

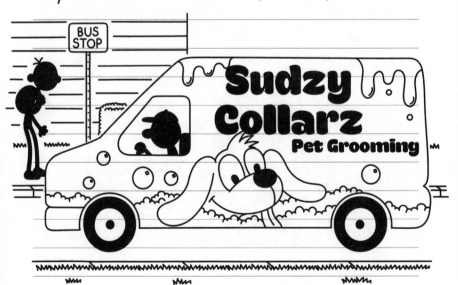

And even though I like dogs, I'm the type of person who needs their space in the morning.

I tried to tell myself it wasn't so bad. But that was before one of the groomers washed a big Saint Bernard, and he shook himself off mid-rinse.

If you ask me, the first day at a new school is hard enough without smelling like a wet dog.

I thought there might be some kind of official welcome for the new students, but I'm not so sure anyone even knew we were coming. I'm kind of glad they didn't make a big deal of it, though, because I got some hard looks when I walked down the hallway.

At least I was smart enough not to wear any gear from my old school. Andrew Huck had on a Looters shirt, and he might as well have been wearing a target on his back.

Nobody gave us a schedule, so when the bell rang I stepped into the nearest classroom, where the English teacher was reading a picture book that was way below our grade level.

That's when I started to realize that the quality of education was even lower at this school than it was at the one I came from.

In Social Studies, they were using textbooks that were at least twenty years old. In Geometry, they were going over stuff we covered a REALLY long time ago.

In Science, they had the same type of equipment we had at our school. But I'm pretty sure they were just burning stuff for fun.

That wasn't the only thing that was a little off, though. In Phys Ed, they used full-size softballs for the Dodgeball unit. The Special of the Day in the cafeteria was a fried fish patty between two slices of pepperoni pizza. And even though the school assembly was entertaining, it didn't seem to have any actual educational value.

So I'm trying not to get too comfortable here. Because based on my experiences on the first day, I'd be willing to bet Slacksville is going to be the next school to close.

Friday

The nice thing about being in a place where the expectations are a little lower is that it gives you a chance to shine. And not to brag, but I'm pretty sure I'm one of the smartest kids at my new school.

People are starting to notice, too. I overheard a kid asking his friend how much time was left in class, so I told him. And they were both amazed I knew how to read a regular clock.

Word got around, and now everyone at school is calling me Time Lord. I don't know if I should be proud of knowing how to tell the time, but I guess when you're the new kid you need to take what you can get.

But then my fame reached a whole new level. We were making fudge brownies in Home Ec, and when I looked in the fridge to see what other ingredients they had, I realized I could whip something up that would guarantee me an A in the class.

So that's how fudgedogs got introduced to Slacksville Middle School. And even though I felt kind of bad for giving away my old school's secret recipe, I figured it didn't really matter anymore.

The clock thing made me popular, but the fudgedogs made me FAMOUS. And now all of a sudden I had a TON of new friends in the cafeteria.

But the best part was when I started getting a few female admirers, which never happened at my old school.

I noticed a couple of girls were whispering about me in the hallway, and then one named Sophie came over and asked a question. And even though I could tell she was just looking for an excuse to talk, I didn't really mind.

Things moved pretty fast from there. Sophie and I ate lunch together for the rest of the week, and when she held my hand in the hallway, that made it official.

But even though I'm really enjoying what the two of us have going on at school, it won't really mean anything until we go on an actual date to the movies or something. Because we're starting to run out of things to talk about at lunch, and there are only so many fudgedogs a person can eat.

SMACK
CHOMP CHEW

Saturday

I worked up the nerve to ask Sophie to go out on a date, and she said yes. But since neither one of us can drive, that meant we'd have to get one of our parents to do it.

I really didn't want either of my parents driving, because I knew they'd totally embarrass me in front of a girl. So Sophie asked her dad to take us to the movies, and he said he would.

I waited out in my front yard, and when I saw a car driving slowly down our street I knew it must be them. And one look at her dad's fancy car told me their family must have a lot of money.

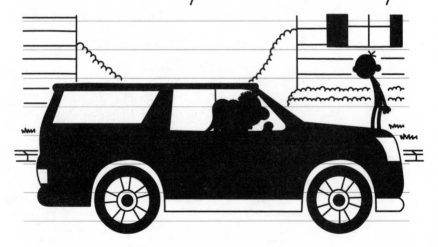

I saw the car's license plate before I noticed who was driving it. And that's when I realized I'd never asked Sophie her last name.

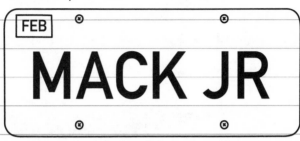

Sophie never mentioned that her dad was Larry Mack Junior, and if she had, I probably wouldn't have had the courage to ask her out. But now here he was, in front of my house. And he didn't look too thrilled to be there, either.

It turns out Sophie didn't tell her dad what town I lived in before she asked him to pick me up, and that might've actually been on purpose. Because from the way he was acting, he didn't seem too thrilled to be in a neighborhood on the other side of the tracks.

I'd never met someone as famous as Larry Mack Junior, so I was a little nervous. I tried to talk to him about car stuff, but I probably made myself sound dumb.

When we got to the movie theater, he actually came inside with us. And I'm not sure if he really wanted to see the movie or if he was just there to keep an eye on us.

After the movie, we went to a place that sells burgers and shakes. I was hoping Sophie's dad would wait in the car, but he followed us in THERE, too.

As soon as we sat down, Larry Mack Junior started grilling me. He wanted to know what kinds of kids I hung out with and what my parents did for a living, and even what kind of car they drove. It was pretty clear he didn't think a person like me was good enough for his daughter.

Luckily, I got a break when the waiter came to the table to hand us our menus. It took me a second to recognize him, though.

It was Mr. Leyton, my old Latin teacher. I was a little surprised to see him working in a place like this, but I was just happy to see a friendly face.

We got into a conversation, and all my Latin came rushing back. After we made small talk about the weather and stuff like that, I placed an order for three hamburgers and three chocolate milkshakes, which really seemed to impress Sophie's dad.

All of a sudden, Larry Mack Junior started acting totally different toward me. Now he wanted to know about what kind of student I was and if I had any OTHER talents I could share with him.

Sophie told her dad I could tell the time using a real clock, which unfortunately didn't seem to impress him as much as it did my classmates at Slacksville Middle School.

Then she told him that I invented fudgedogs, which DID seem to impress him. So for the rest of the night we just talked about what it takes to run a successful business.

I don't want to get too ahead of myself, but if this thing works out with Sophie my future might be totally different. And I'd definitely be willing to change my last name if that's what it took to be a part of the family business.

TELL 'EM THE MACKS SENT YA!

Sophie Mack

Gregory Mack

Gregory Mack Junior

<u>Monday</u>
A lot has changed since my date with Sophie, and none of it is good for me.

Larry Mack Junior decided the reason I was such a bright kid was because of the education I received at Larry Mack Middle School. So he donated a ton of money to reopen it, but this time with a new name.

The Student Crier

SAVED!
Millionaire Rescues Shuttered School

LARRY MACK JUNIOR
MIDDLE SCHOOL

He even updated the statue in the front courtyard to mark the reopening.

Even though it cost Larry Mack Junior a fortune to reopen the school, he got his money back right away. That's because when the workers started renovations in the C wing, they discovered bags of cash in the walls.

RRRRRRRR

When the school reopened, me and all the kids who got sent to Slacksville and Fulson Tech had to come back. And not everyone was thrilled about the news.

In fact, I think most people were HAPPY at their new schools. So all of a sudden I'm the villain for getting our school reopened.

Sophie didn't want to date long-distance, so when I switched schools she broke up with me. But I'm thinking I might've actually dodged a bullet on that one.

> Dear Greg—
>
> It's ovor.

I still see her dad almost every day, though. I guess I inspired him to go back to school and complete his education, so now he's in half my classes.

And he must have a lot of pull with the school, because he managed to get Mr. Leyton rehired.

Larry Mack Junior doesn't go to school full-time because he's still got a car dealership to run. And apparently it's doing better than ever with their new promotion.

Speaking of which, now the town of Slacksville is claiming that THEY invented fudgedogs, and they even put up a new billboard.

In fact, Slacksville patented the recipe, which means we're not allowed to sell fudgedogs in our cafeteria anymore. Lately, our school's been trying out some new food items, but so far nothing's really taken off.

When the school reopened, they tried to get Principal Bottoms to come back to finish out the year. But from what I've heard, he's got a place in the Caribbean and he's enjoying his new life.

So they hired a temporary replacement until they find someone permanent. But if they end up sticking with the new guy, I have serious concerns about where my education is headed.

ACKNOWLEDGMENTS

Thanks to every librarian for your dedication to connecting kids with books that help shape them into the people they will become. More than ever, your work is vital and so appreciated by every author who's ever written a book.

Thanks to my wife, Julie, for your love and support. Thanks to Jess Brallier for helping me get started as an author. And thanks to Charlie Kochman for being such a wonderful partner in this journey.

Thanks to Mary O'Mara and Steve Roman for making this book the best it could be. Thanks to everyone at Abrams, especially Mary McAveney, Andrew Smith, Elisa Gonzalez, Pamela Notarantonio, Lora Grisafi, Hallie Patterson, Melanie Chang, Kim Lauber, Alison Gervais, Erin Vandeveer, and Borana Greku. Special thanks to Michael Jacobs for all your support over the years, and best wishes for your adventures ahead!

Thanks to the Wimpy Kid team—Anna Cesary, Vanessa Jedrej, Shaelyn Germain, and Colleen Regan—for making work so much fun!

Thanks to the wonderful team at An Unlikely Story and to Rich Carr, Andrea Lucey, Paul Sennott, Sylvie Rabineau, and Keith Fleer.

Thanks to everyone at Disney, especially Roland Poindexter, Michael Musgrave, Kathryn Jones, Ralph Milera, and Vanessa Morrison.

ABOUT THE AUTHOR

Jeff Kinney is a #1 *New York Times* bestselling author and a six-time Nickelodeon Kids' Choice Award winner for Favorite Book. Jeff has been named one of *Time* magazine's 100 Most Influential People in the World. He spent his childhood in the Washington, D.C., area and later moved to New England, where he and his family own a bookstore called An Unlikely Story.